University of Buckingham Press, 51 Gower Street, London, WC1E 6HJ
info@unibuckinghampress.com | www.unibuckinghampress.com

Text and Illustrations © Wendy Goucher, 2021
Illustrations by Jim Barker, 2021

The right of the above author to be identified as the author of this work has been asserted in accordance with the Copyright, Designs and Patents Act 1988. British Library Cataloguing in Publication Data available.

Print: 9781800316218
Ebook: 9781800316225

Set in Aniara. Printing managed by Jellyfish Solutions Ltd

All characters, other than those clearly in the public domain, and place names, other than those well-established such as towns and cities, are fictitious and any resemblance is purely coincidental.

All rights reserved. No part of this publication may be reproduced, stored in or introduced into a retrieval system, or transmitted, in any form, or by any means electronic, mechanical, photocopying, recording or otherwise, without the prior permission of the publisher. Any person who commits any unauthorised act in relation to this publication may be liable to criminal prosecution and civil claims for damages.

OXFORDSHIRE COUNTY COUNCIL	
3303671347	
Askews & Holts	27-Aug-2021
JF	

Which One is Nettie?

Book 2 of Nettie's Internet Safety Books

Wendy Goucher

illustrated by Jim Barker

Nettie loves to play games on her Grandad's tablet. Her favourite game takes her into Cyberland.

When she wants to play she has to ask Grandad first, and he uses his top-secret password to unlock the tablet for her.

Grandad says the top-secret password is like a key.
It stops people using the tablet without permission.

One day Nettie showed Charlie, Grandad's dog, lots of pictures of Cyberland on the tablet.

He loved to see the fairground and the lovely green grass, and of course the funny bunnies.

"Uncle Alfred, the head bunny has invited me and Webby to a bunny picnic party," said Nettie.

Charlie barked in excitement. "Please, please take me to the picnic," said Charlie.

"Don't be silly, Charlie", Nettie said "Dogs can't go to Cyberland."

9

Then the doorbell rang and Nettie jumped down to answer the door. She loves to take the parcels from the delivery person.

Nettie was in so much of a hurry that she forgot to lock the tablet. While she was gone Charlie jumped back up on the table and looked at the tablet.

"There's Cyberland," he thought, and he sniffed at the screen so much he had his nose on the screen.

Then he sniffed a little more and his nose went through the screen and he followed behind.

Because Nettie helped to unwrap the parcel she and Webby were late to the picnic.

Uncle Alfred was waiting for them when they arrived.

"Come quick," he said, "before the cake is all gone."

As they got closer they could hear the bunnies chatting and laughing.

But then they saw something very odd.

It looked like Webby was already there.

"Look, Uncle Alfred," said a bunny on the left, "Nettie and Webby are here."

"But Nettie and Webby are already here," said a bunny on the right.

The picnic was still.

The picnic was silent.

Nobody knew what to do.

Then Charlie sneezed.

Uncle Alfred raised his finger and pointed at Charlie.

"You're not Nettie!" he said. "Catch them!" he yelled.

So Charlie and his Webby ran and the bunnies ran after them.

Nettie and Webby looked down at the picnic. The other Webby's arm had fallen in the cake and made a big mess.

Nettie was very sad.

Nettie was also very cross with Charlie for spoiling the picnic.

When Nettie and Webby got back to her grandparents' house Nettie told them the whole story.

When Charlie tried to creep out to the garden, Grandma caught him.

"You are a very naughty dog, Charlie," Grandma said.
"You spoilt Nettie's picnic with the bunnies."

Charlie nuzzled Nettie to try to say sorry, but she was still upset.

Then Grandad said, "Nettie, although Charlie was wrong to spoil your picnic, it is partly your fault. Why was Charlie able to get into Cyberland?"

Nettie thought.
Then Nettie remembered.

"I didn't lock the tablet when I went to get the parcel. That is why Charlie could be there."

"That's right," said Grandma. "It is not all his fault".

Nettie got down from the table and stroked Charlie's head.

Charlie tried to lick her face – he was very sorry.

Nettie giggled. "OK, Charlie, I am sorry too."

A little while later Grandad and Grandma and Nettie and Charlie all went to the park. Nettie and Charlie played fetch with a ball until they were both tired.

Later Grandad made a cake, a carrot cake of course, and Nettie had some for her supper.

So, Nettie went to bed and dreamt of bunnies and picnics and a big, tasty cake – and so did Charlie.

So, what do you think?

What is the name of the bunny in the big hat?

Why were the rabbits puzzled when Nettie and Webby arrived at the picnic?

How did the bunnies realised that Charlie was only pretending to be Nettie?

Let's talk

Why was Charlie able to get into Cyberland?

When a tablet or computer is locked up how can you open it again?

Why are passwords important?

A Message for Parents, Family Members and Carers

One of the most important purposes of this book is to give you the chance to talk with the small child in your care about the Internet, the problems and concerns. You will need to talk to them about it someday, so starting now is a good time.

If you feel you would like more information about keeping young children safe online, there are a number of websites that can answer your questions and give you good advice.

These include:

Think U Know: guidance and resources for professionals, families and children. www.thinkuknow.co.uk

National Crime Agency's command for Child Exploitation and Online Protection
www.ceop.police.uk/safety-centre

Information and advice on complaints procedures and reporting routes to social media providers about inappropriate content can be accessed at www.reportharmfulcontent.com

www.saferinternet.org.uk

www.stopitnow.org.uk/scotland

South West Grid for Learning: www.swgfl.org.uk/online-safety

www.nspcc.org.uk/keeping-children-safe/online-safety

www.getsafeonline.org and www.ncsc.gov.uk

www.young.scot/campaigns/national/digiaye

www.scotland.police.uk/youth-hub

Lightning Source UK Ltd.
Milton Keynes UK
UKHW051141290721
387914UK00004B/35